For Oscar

First published 2006 by Walker Books Ltd 87 Vauxhall Walk, London SE11 5HJ   2 4 6 8 10 9 7 5 3 1   © 2006 Niamh Sharkey   The right of Niamh Sharkey to be identified as author/illustrator of this work has been asserted by her in accordance with the Copyright, Designs and Patents Act 1988   This book has been typeset in Sharkey.   Printed in China.   All rights reserved.   British Library Cataloguing in Publication Data: a catalogue record for this book is available from the British Library   ISBN-13: 978-1-84428-049-0 (hb)   ISBN-13: 978-1-4063-0396-4 (pb)   www.walkerbooks.co.uk

I'm a Happy Hugglewug

Niamh Sharkey

WALKER BOOKS
AND SUBSIDIARIES
LONDON • BOSTON • SYDNEY • AUCKLAND

My Hugglewug Song

Oh, oh, oh...
I'm a Hugglewug and I'm happy.
I jump in the air.
I've got twirly whirly horns
and spikey spikey hair.
I wriggle my fingers
and twiddle my toes.
Between my shiny shiny
eyes is my sniffy
sniffy nose.

My mouth is wibbly wobbly.

My tongue is this l... o... n... g...

My Hugglewug Family

My brother Cobby

Baby Ivor's teddy

My baby brother Ivor

My sister Lola

My mummy

My pet fish Horace

Me (Henry)

My daddy

My nanny

My grandaddy

Start the Day the Hugglewug Way!

Baby Ivor loves his porridge.

Gurgle wurgle

I love hugging Mummy.

Lola loves dancing after breakfast.

Cobby and Daddy love reading.

Come and Meet My Hugglewug Friends!

1, 2, 3,
we're off to school!

Hey! There's Oscar
chasing Denzel.
Go, go, guys!

Gertie is
skipping.

I see Mini and Max
on the slide.

Bang that drum,
Ruby!

Jump over that
mushroom, Meg!

Splash! Splosh!
Stanley is in a puddle.

It's Time for Hugglewug School!

Here comes a Hugglewug through the window,

here comes a Hugglewug through the door.

Here comes a Hugglewug round the corner,

Hugglewugs! Hugglewugs! Hugglewugs! At Hugglewug School we learn to ...

The Scary Hugglewug Counting Game

1 Little

2 Little

4 Little

5 Little

7 Little

8 Little

9 Little Hugglewugs

3 Little Hugglewugs

6 Little Hugglewugs

10 Little Hugglewugs ...

CAN'T SCARE

ME!

Let's All Paint a Picture!

Scribble!

Cobby is drawing a scary blue monster.

Splosh!

Look! Lola's dancing with a paintbrush.

Squelch!

Ruby loves being messy.

Squirt!

Careful with that red paint, Denzel!

What a
lovely
picture!

Climb the Hugglewug Tree!

It's after school — yippee yippee!
Time to play before our tea.

Hugglewugs! Hugglewugs! Up a tree!
How many Hugglewugs can you see?

I Spy Hugglewug Pie

Muffin

Carrot

Hugglewug pie

Apple

Glass of lemonade

Fork

Knife

Hugglebug

Spoon

Worm

Hugglewug cake

Yellow mushroom

Red mushroom

Snail

Peas

Popcorn

Plate

Our Hugglewug Animal Friends

Woof

Woof

Nibble nibble

There are Lola and Hugglewug dog.

Oink oink

Hugglewug rabbit loves to munch on carrots.

Baby Ivor is playing snap with Hugglewug pig.

Lola
is so
wuggly!

I'm so
snuggly!

Baby
is so
Hugglewuggly!

My Hugglewug Lullaby

I see the moon,
the moon sees me.

Hugglewug moon!
Hugglewug me!

Between my shiny shiny eyes is my sniffy sniffy nose.

My mouth is wibbly wobbly.

My tongue is this l... o... n... g...

S: **Come on, everybody! Sing our Hugglewug Song!**

Oh, oh, oh...